MY AUNTIE IS
A LITTLE BIT BONKERS

My auntie is a little bit bonkers, you know...

Come and meet her and say hello!

She goes to the desert for her holidays...

To have some fun and catch the sun's rays.

She travels around in a hot air balloon...

And sometimes ventures up to the moon.

She's cool and hip and when she gets sleepy...

She goes to bed in a cozy tepee.

She eats ice cream with a chocolate flake...

Her pet chameleon likes to eat cake!

She jumps over rainbows, right up to the sun...

My bonkers auntie is so much fun!

She lives in a palace all fancy and bright...

And has lots of balloons so colorful and light.

She has a pet llama with legs rather wonky...

She has a pet lion, a croc and a monkey!

She bakes the best cakes and makes fancy tea...

When I'm with my auntie such fun she can be!

She wears groovy dresses and bunny ears...

When I'm sad she wipes my tears.

She has a cool garden with birds and flowers...

PLANTS

When I go to auntie's I could stay there for hours.

She loves to smell flowers she likes butterflies too...

I'm so glad I have an
auntie like you.

Made in the USA
Las Vegas, NV
07 November 2024